Seedling
& Sprout™
GROWING WITH GOD

THE LONG SHORTCUT

WRITTEN & ILLUSTRATED
BY THE DE VILLIERS FAMILY

WATERBROOK
PRESS

THE LONG SHORTCUT
PUBLISHED BY WATERBROOK PRESS
12265 Oracle Boulevard, Suite 200
Colorado Springs, Colorado 80921
A division of Random House, Inc.

ISBN 1-4000-7195-X

Published in association with the literary agency of Alive Communications, Inc., 7680 Goddard Street, Suite 200, Colorado Springs, CO 80920.

Library of Congress Cataloging-in-Publication Data

The long shortcut : a Sprout story / written and
illustrated by the de Villiers Family.
    p. cm. — (Sprout growing with God)
  Summary: Twig is late for school one day, so he disobeys the rules,
  takes a shortcut, and gets lost in the woods.
  ISBN 1-4000-7195-X
  [1. Behavior—Fiction. 2. Lost children—Fiction. 3.
  Schools—Fiction.] I. Series.
PZ7.L8594 2006
[E]—dc22
                                    2005026532

Printed in China
2006—First Edition

10 9 8 7 6 5 4 3 2 1

Sprout was dreaming of ice-cream sundaes when he heard his mother's voice calling him. His eyes popped open. The morning sun shone brightly through his bedroom window. "What time is it?" he thought, as he sprang out of bed.

"Oh no," he said aloud, "I'm going to be late for school. I didn't even hear the La-dee-da birds sing their wake-up call, this morning."

He got ready as quickly as he could, called goodbye to his mom, ran out of the door, and whizzed down the slide to the bottom of his tree home. Twig and Petal, his two best friends, were waiting for him.

"Come on, we're going to be late," they both yelled, as he landed at their feet. "You know that Mr. Nectar will wonder where we are."

"I'm sorry. I slept in too late. We'll just have to run as fast as we can," Sprout answered breathlessly. The three set off down the path.

Suddenly Twig stopped. "Wait, I know a shortcut. Follow me."

Sprout and Petal stared at him. "You know we can't do that," they said. "We are not allowed to take any other path to school. Mr. Nectar told us to always stay on this path."

"Yeah, but we'll be late," argued Twig.

"I'd rather be late than disobey our teacher," said Sprout. Petal nodded her head in agreement.

"I bet I'll be at school before you," said Twig, as he turned off the path.

"Please come back," Sprout and Petal called, but Twig took no notice of them.

They watched as he disappeared around the corner, then they hurried on their way to school.

moments after they arrived at school, the bell rang. They looked around the room, but there was no sign of Twig. "I can't believe he's not here yet," Petal whispered.

"Shhh," said Sprout, "Don't tell anyone what happened."

Then Mr. Nectar came into the room and everyone stopped talking.

"Good morning students," he said, looking around.

"Today we are going to learn about how plants grow." He paused. "Where is Twig this morning?"

Sprout stared down at his desk, but when he looked up Mr. Nectar was standing right next to him.

"Have you seen Twig today?"

"I think he'll be here soon," Sprout mumbled.

"I hope so," Mr. Nectar said.

Meanwhile, just as Twig started to wonder if he'd gone the right way, he noticed strange voices were coming toward him. A group of older kids appeared on the pathway. His heart pounded in his ears.

"Hey, look at the little kid," one of them said. "What's your name, kid? Where are you going?"

They came closer and closer to Twig. They were very BIG. Twig felt as though he was going to faint and his legs shook like leaves.

"I'm on my way to school," he said quietly.

"What did you say?" asked the biggest kid. Twig was so frightened that he turned and ran away as fast as his shaky legs could go.

"Hey! Come back here," they called, but he didn't stop.

He hid in an old tree stump until it was quiet. Slowly he crawled out and looked around. The older kids were gone.

He got up and started walking again in one direction, but it didn't look right. So he tried the other way. That didn't look right either.

He didn't know which way to go.

Twig was hopelessly lost!

Back at school, it was recess and everyone was playing outside. Only Sprout didn't feel like playing today. He was worried about Twig. Where could he be?

"Sprout, is something wrong?" asked Mr. Nectar.

Sprout took a deep breath. "Twig took a shortcut to school this morning and he's not here yet and I'm scared that something has happened to him," he said in a rush.

His teacher frowned. "A shortcut? Why didn't you tell me this before, Sprout?"

Sprout's head hung low. "Well, come along then.
We had better go and look for him."

Sprout and Mr. Nectar went
back down the path until they
came to the place where Twig
had gone his own way.

"He went that way," said Sprout, pointing in the other direction. They hurried down the path.

They passed the Dooberry Bogs,
and stopped to ask the dooberry
pickers if they had seen Twig.
They hadn't.

Next they met Auntie Moss carrying a large basket of fresh dooberry muffins to market. "Have you seen Twig," Mr. Nectar asked.

"Sorry, I haven't," she answered. "Would you like a muffin?"

Sprout and Mr. Nectar kept looking.
Searching behind rocks and trees, under
bushes, and everywhere they could think
of, but Twig was nowhere.

Sprout grew more and more worried that something bad might have happened.

Sprout's legs were getting very tired. "Please, can we rest for a little while?" he asked. So they sat down beside the path and the forest grew quiet. Suddenly Sprout stood up.
"What is that sound?" he asked.
"It sounds like someone crying!"

Sprout forgot about his tired
legs and ran down the path,
with Mr. Nectar right behind.

Around the corner, sitting
in the middle of the path by
himself, was Twig. He looked
very unhappy. Sprout was so
relieved to see him that he
ran up and gave Twig a big hug.
"I'm so glad we found you,"
exclaimed Sprout.

"we were worried about you,
Twig," Mr. Nectar added. "Is
everything okay?"

"I was lost and some big kids showed up. I was scared, so I ran away, but I didn't know which way to go," Twig replied.

"Why did you go off on your own like that?" Mr. Nectar said. "You know it's against the rules."

"I know," answered Twig. "But I thought I knew a better way. I guess was wrong. I'm so sorry, Mr. Nectar."

"And I'm sorry, too," added Sprout. "I should have told you the truth before."

Mr. Nectar looked at Twig and smiled. "Perhaps you understand better why it's important to follow the rules? I'm sure Petal will be happy to see you. Listen, if we race back to school, we'll be just in time for lunch. The winner can have extra dessert!"

And the three set off running down the path back to school.

thinklings

1.

How did Twig disobey the rules?

2.

What happened to Twig when he went his own way?

3.

Why is it important to always be obedient?

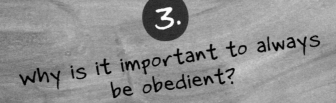

BE CAREFUL TO OBEY SO THAT
ALL MAY GO WELL WITH YOU.
DEUTERONOMY 6:3